KU-167-077

Nothing Can
Separate Us

Nothing Can Separate Us

THE STORY OF NAN HARPER

By Tracy M. Leininger

NOTHING CAN SEPARATE US
Published by His Seasons
Copyright © 2000
All rights reserved

Layout and Design by Joshua Goforth and Noelle Wheeler
Illustrations by Kelly Pulley and Lisa Reed
Production Coordinator Cathy Craven

Scripture taken from the King James Version and
the New King James Version © 1982 Thomas Nelson Publishers

No portion of this book may be reproduced in any form
without the written permission of the publisher.

Printed in the United States of America by Jostens Commercial Publications
ISBN 1-929241-21-6

HIS SEASONS™

8122 Datapoint Drive
Suite 900
San Antonio, TX 78229
(210) 490-2101
www.hisseasons.com

To my cousin, Peter Leininger, who has a love for the Lord and a passion to see the lost come to a saving knowledge of Christ. Peter's example has inspired and challenged me to strive for the same.

✦ ✦ ✦ ✦ ✦ ✦ ✦ ✦ ✦ ✦ ✦ ✦ ✦

To Doug Phillips, who has devoted his life to passing on an enduring legacy of faith to future generations and who has rekindled the vision of "women and children first."

✦ ✦ ✦ ✦ ✦ ✦ ✦ ✦ ✦

To these devoted fathers and men of God, I dedicate this book.

CHAPTER ONE

Looking Back from the Shores of Ireland

"Mother, do tell me about the time you were rescued from the *Titanic*," little Gordon pleaded as he looked up from the small boat that he was holding. "And tell me of Grandfather Harper and how he helped the people when the ship was sinking. I am about to launch my little ship, and I would love to hear the story again!"

Leaving their Scottish home, Nan and her husband, Reverend Philip Roy Pont, were enjoying a quiet summer holiday in Queenstown, Ireland. It was there, off Roche's Point, that *Titanic* last made anchorage. After picking up more passengers and cargo, the great ship had embarked on her maiden voyage.

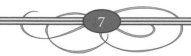

Even though many years had passed, the memories were still fresh in Nan's mind. She strolled through the emerald hills that rolled into the deep blue-green sea, breathing deeply of the fresh ocean breeze. It seemed like just yesterday that *Titanic* left Ireland's shores.

If it were not for the presence of her young son, Gordon, she might have felt that she was once again a little six-year-old girl, standing hand in hand with her father, Reverend John Harper, on the deck of *Titanic*.

Nan smiled at the happy memories of those first days aboard ship. Sitting down on a moss-covered rock, she pondered the events of her voyage aboard *Titanic*—a ship whose destiny had changed the course of her life. Looking far out to sea, she seemed totally absorbed in her thoughts. Then, taking a deep breath, Nan began the gripping story in her Scottish accent.

+ + + + + + + + + + + +

Father, Auntie Jessie, and I stood on the deck of the great ship, *Titanic*. It was April 11, 1912. I eagerly watched as rows of tenders* left the Irish shores, bringing new passengers eager to board the illustrious ship. The wee tenders looked like your toy boat, and the passengers looked like tiny ants in comparison to the enormous steamer we were on.

"Look Father!" I exclaimed, my eyes sparkling with excitement. "What pretty Irish lace and linens those bumboats** are carrying. I do love bonny*** things and this ship is full of them."

"Aye, my lassie, just think of it," Father said, with his tender smile that always warmed the depths of my heart. "If man can create such beauty on earth, how much more glorious are the mansions our Father has prepared for us in Heaven! Think, Nan, your dear mother is already there, rejoicing with

*tender—a small vessel employed to serve or attend a larger vessel
**bumboat—a small boat, for carrying provisions
***bonny—beautiful

the angels in that heavenly home. Can your wee imagination see that she is in a much more beautiful place?"

"Is it more lovely than the fashionable first-class lounge and dining salon?" I questioned. "And what about the staircase with the glass-domed skylight? I thought that to be lovely, indeed. Can heaven be more beautiful than that?"

Though we were second-class passengers, we were allowed to tour first-class before *Titanic* left England. I had never seen such elegance. There were marble floors, golden light fixtures, crystal chandeliers, and the most beautiful paintings in elegantly carved frames. Oh, and how can I forget the heated indoor swimming pool. They even had Turkish baths, to boot!

"Aye, heaven is far more dazzling, dear," Father said with the light of God's love shining in his eyes.

Father so loved God that his whole face radiated with joy when he spoke of Him. From my earliest years, I remember Father telling others about Christ. Whether he preached from the pulpit or cared for a drunk on the street, he proclaimed the way of salvation. We had been on the boat only one day, yet Father had already made many new friends. He told them of Christ's love and encouraged them to think of their eternal destiny.

Crowds gathered at the shoreline to see *Titanic* leave the harbor, and as the enormous engines were started, I could feel the ship rumble. Pulling up anchor, we left the Irish shores behind. Smoke billowed out of the four great smokestacks as we headed toward the frigid North Atlantic. The White Star Line boasted that *Titanic* would make it to New York City in record time.

During the first few days, I spent many joyful hours with Father. He would scoop me into his lap and tell me many of his childhood stories. One time, at the age of two, he almost drowned after falling into a garden well. Another time, he and my Uncle George started a mission project together. "The

Harper Brothers" ministry was almost completely wiped out when a swift ocean current carried them away.

My favorite story was the time he went sailing in the Mediterranean Sea. The splendid journey took a sudden turn when the ship sprang a leak and began to founder. "The fear of death did not for one moment disturb me," Father said. "I knew that sudden death would be sudden glory. But," he added, placing a kiss on my forehead, "there was a wee motherless girl in Glasgow who needed me." My father's tender thoughtfulness filled my heart with glee.

"That's my favorite part of the story," I exclaimed, throwing my arms around Father's neck and hugging him tight. I always knew that I was Father's wee princess. How I loved to hear his stories!

It was now three days into the voyage. Traveling blissfully over the tranquil seas, I thought I was as near heaven as possible. To add to my enjoyment,

Auntie Jessie introduced me to another wee lass who was just a year older than myself. Her name was Eva Hart and we soon became constant playmates.

"I have a lovely plan," Eva announced with her proper English accent. "Let us have a tea party with my teddy bear. We can pretend that we are some of the elegant ladies in first-class. You can be the Countess of Rothes, since she, too, is Scottish. I shall be Edith Evans, a brilliant American woman with whom my mother spoke when we toured first-class."

Since I had been raised on Father's small minister's salary, I was not accustomed to fine tea parties. But, whenever Father gave me permission to play, I took great delight in our "elegant" teas.

It was in this way that we spent the first part of our journey. My Father kept busy urging the unsaved aboard ship to gain an eternal perspective. I did not see my auntie much during the day, but we shared a cabin together. In the

evenings I would excitedly tell her all about the events of the day. Little did I know, however, that each passing sunset drew us closer to the perilous ice fields of the North Atlantic.

Fear not, for I am with you;

be not dismayed, for I am your God.

I will strengthen you, yes, I will help you,

I will uphold you with My righteous right hand.

Isaiah 41:10

CHAPTER TWO

O God, Our Help in Ages Past

The next morning was Sunday, April 14, and I eagerly dressed for the worship service. From a young age, I loved to sing and listen as the Scriptures were read. I was especially thrilled that morning, because, just before our journey, the kind members of our church in Glasgow had given me a fashionable pink dress. They felt I should have a first-rate dress if I was going to accompany my father on his trip to America. He was to preach at the Moody Bible Institute in Chicago. As I slipped the dress over my head, I felt that it was the loveliest I had ever worn!

"Nan!" Father said, "What have we here? Ye look like a wee highland princess in that dress."

Taking my hand, he led me to the second-class dining salon, where the service was to be held. Reginald Barker, Captain Smith's assistant purser,* conducted the worship. My friend, Eva Hart, was thrilled when they began to sing her favorite hymn, *O God, Our Help In Ages Past.* I'll never forget her smile as we both sang out wholeheartedly.

> *O God, our Help in ages past,*
> *Our Hope for years to come,*
> *Our Shelter from the stormy blast,*
> *And our eternal Home!*
>
> *Under the shadow of Thy throne*
> *Still may we dwell secure;*
> *Sufficient is Thine arm alone,*
> *And our defense is sure.*

*purser—a ship's officer in charge of accounts, freights, or tickets.

O God, our Help in ages past,
Our Hope for years to come,
Be Thou our Guide while life shall last,
And our eternal Home.

Outside, the air was growing cold, and the waters were growing colder still, but there, within *Titanic*, our hearts could not have been warmer.

Later on, as Eva and I walked back to our rooms, she told me of a conversation she had overheard.

"Last night," Eva began with wide eyes, "I was having a hard time going to sleep. Then I heard Mother speaking with Father in hushed tones. She said that the White Star Line had declared *Titanic*, 'unsinkable,' and that someone had gone as far as to say that not even *God* could sink this ship! Ever since then, she has felt uneasy about the journey." Eva continued in a serious tone. "Mother says that it is not wise to tempt God like that. She has not been able to sleep at night for fear that we might sink!" Realizing her words had troubled Nan, she added, "I was glad when we sang my favorite hymn in service today. It helped me remember to not be afraid."

Eva was seven, just a year older than I, but I looked up to her as if she were much older. I took her words very seriously and spent the rest of the day trying not to worry. I also told Auntie Jessie of my concerns, and though she encouraged me to not be afraid, I could not get rid of the sick feeling in my stomach. I knew I must talk to Father about it just as soon as we were alone.

That evening as couples were waltzing to Strauss in the ballroom, Father was up on deck leading a deckhand to Christ. I always enjoyed listening to Father as he spoke of his Savior. He was so intense, yet so joyful and kindhearted—a true Scotsman.

✦ ✦ ✦ ✦ ✦ ✦ ✦ ✦ ✦ ✦ ✦ ✦ ✦

Nan smiled, and taking her gaze away from the distant horizon she looked at her young son. "Yes, a true Scotsman indeed, just like you are going to be when you grow up, Gordon."

Throughout the story, Gordon had listened with rapt attention. Though he had heard the story many times, never had his mother shared so much detail.

"Please, do go on, Mother," Gordon pleaded, unable to bear the suspense. "You were saying that you and Grandfather Harper were on the deck of *Titanic* and that you had not yet talked with him about your fear of the boat sinking."

"Aye, that's right." Nan's gaze returned to sea, but her thoughts took her far beyond.

✦ ✦ ✦ ✦ ✦ ✦ ✦ ✦ ✦ ✦ ✦ ✦ ✦

CHAPTER THREE

"It Will Be Beautiful in the Morning"

That evening the soft music, which streamed out from the ballroom, seemed to calm the water below. The sun melted into the placid sea and its brilliant rays shot into the sky above, bidding the world goodnight.

"Well Jessie, just ye look at this lovely evening! It will be beautiful in the morning," Father said to Auntie as we all turned to go below deck to our cabins.

After I had slipped my warmest nightgown over my head, Father tucked me in bed and led our family devotions. He opened his Bible to Psalm 139 and read, "Thou hast beset me behind and before, and laid Thine hand upon me . . . If I take the wings of the morning, and dwell in the uttermost parts of the sea; even there Thy hand shall lead me, and Thy right hand shall hold me." These verses penetrated into the very depths of my heart. Then I remembered what Eva told me.

"Father!" I exclaimed. "What if the ship were to sink? How could God's hand guide us then?" I quickly told him all Eva Hart had related to me. Father agreed that it was, indeed, a very foolish thing to tempt God.

"But, I have something to show ye which I think might give your wee heart some rest," Father said, leading me to the porthole window of our cabin. "Look up at the heavens. What do ye see, lass?"

Night had fallen, and thousands of bright stars illuminated the sky. Despite the light from the boat, I saw many more stars than I had ever seen back home in Glasgow. It looked as though the angels in heaven had opened

all the windows of glory to give us a tiny glimpse of the splendors beyond.

"There are not only more stars than ye could ever count," Father continued, "but when ye look through a telescope, there are thousands more than your natural eye can see. And yet—" Father paused. He, too, was filled with awe, "and yet, our Heavenly Father has crafted each one and knows their number."

"Whenever the cares of this world are heavy upon my heart, I often look up at the sky and remember that the God who fashioned the starry heavens is the same God who created me. There is nothing too great for Him and nothing too small." Father looked lovingly into my eyes and continued, "Nan, ye need not ever fear. God's Word says He has loved you with an everlasting love, and nothing can separate you from the love of Christ—nothing! Even in death there is victory if you have the Father's love."

Father tucked me back into bed, and we lifted up our hearts to God who held us in His hands. I will never forget the fervency of his prayer that night.

He seemed far away—next to God's throne in the heavenlies, yet at the same time, his prayer made me feel God's presence right there in the room. An indescribable peace filled my young heart, and I drifted off to sleep.

God is our refuge and strength,

a very present help in trouble.

Therefore we will not fear,

even though the earth be removed,

and though the mountains be carried

into the midst of the sea;

though its waters roar and be troubled . . .

Psalm 46:1-3a

CHAPTER FOUR

"S.O.S. Save Our Souls!"

I slept peacefully in the warmth and comfort of my cabin, completely unaware that we were forging through dangerous ice fields. Even though Captain Smith had received several telegraph warnings about the icebergs, he continued at full speed, hoping to make New York Harbor in record time.

Captain Smith, in an attempt to be cautious, instructed the men in the crow's nest to be on the lookout. Though they had seen distant shadows, they sighted nothing alarming.

Then, without warning, it happened.

At 11:40 pm, Frederick Fleet, the ship's lookout, spotted an enormous iceberg directly ahead. He immediately sounded the alarm.

"Iceberg, right ahead!" His urgent voice resounded through the telephone, breaking the serene silence on the bridge.

"Thank you." Sixth Officer James Moody hurriedly replied before passing the message to First Officer Murdoch.

"Hard a-starboard!" Murdoch urgently ordered from the wheelhouse to the engine room. "Stop! Full speed astern!"

But it was too late! Within seconds, *Titanic* struck the iceberg.

An eerie moan resounded through the depths of the freezing waters as the iceberg scraped along the side of the ship, popping rivets and bending the great iron plate. The ship shuddered as water gushed through the opening. Immediately, bells rang out in alarm, indicating to the crew below that the watertight compartment doors were closing.

Not one of the passengers aboard ship realized the extent of the damage, nor the danger we were in. Some of the children, who were on an upper deck, even played with the broken ice that landed there after the collision. But by 12:05 am, Captain Smith knew that the ship and all the passengers were in great danger. He ordered the crew to uncover the lifeboats and urged all passengers to put on their life-vests and await further orders.

Ten minutes later, the wireless operator, Jack Phillips, began sending our first distress call: *"C.Q.D. C.Q.D. C.Q.D. Come Quick, Danger!"* Phillips' assistant soon switched to a new code that had never before been used:

"S.O.S. S.O.S. S.O.S. Save Our Souls!"

By then, the crew realized the gravity of the situation, but they did their best to keep the passengers calm.

I slept soundly through this whole episode, and when Father woke me, it was a little past midnight. He gently shook my shoulder and told me to dress warmly.

As he slipped a life-vest over my head, he said, "Nothing to worry about, dear. The steward has just informed me that they are having a little leak below, and we are to go up top, just to be safe." Picking me up, he assured me with a smile, "After all, the deck will give us a glorious view of the stars."

By the time Auntie Jessie, Father, and I emerged from below, Father realized that things were more serious than he had been led to believe. The ship was tilting slightly toward the bow, and instead of gazing at the peaceful stars, we had to squint into the glare of distress rockets that whistled through the air. People were growing anxious as rumors spread that the "Unsinkable" was slipping into the depths of the icy waters. As the stewards hurriedly loaded the lifeboats, apprehension filled the hearts of many passengers.

Safe in my father's loving arms, I felt no fear or reason for alarm. Yawning, I laid my sleepy head on his shoulder and snuggled deeper into the warmth of his chest. I'll never forget that feeling of peace and security. I often look back and see that moment as a picture of how my Heavenly Father holds us safe in the palm of His loving hand.

Those wonderful moments in his arms passed all too quickly. Father looked deeply into my eyes, and said, "Nan, darling, ye must get into one of the lifeboats with all the women and children, and I must stay on the ship and wait my turn. Do be a brave wee lass and make your Father proud of his princess," he urged tenderly. "And, Nan, dear, no matter what happens to me this night, never forget your Heavenly Father's great love. He will never leave ye. Even if I were to join your mother in glory this night, remember that our home is not here on this earth. It is in heaven, and our parting will be but a brief one. If I make it to glory before ye, I shall be waiting for ye there."

Father hugged me tightly as a tear ran down his cheek. "How I love my wee lassie." Father waited until the last possible moment before handing me to an officer. Quickly bidding Auntie Jessie good-bye, Father helped her into lifeboat number eleven. The officer placed me in my auntie's arms, and the boat began to inch its way down to the dark frigid waters below. Looking back up, I saw Father one last time.

"Woman and children and the unsaved first!" he called out as he helped someone into the next lifeboat. As *Titanic's* wireless operator feverishly tapped out *"S.O.S. Save Our Souls,"* Father thought only of others and was fervently pleading with God to save the eternal souls of the passengers.

. . . I will never leave you nor forsake you . . .

The LORD is my helper; I will not fear.

What can man do to me?

Hebrews 13:5b-6

CHAPTER FIVE

A Still, Cold Night

ur lifeboat jerked and bumped its way down as two crewmen lowered us from the davits.* We were thrown backward and forward as the lifeboat lurched from bow to stern.

"Steady above," a crewman shouted up to the those lowering us down, "or we shall all be thrown into the sea!" The groaning of the davits drowned out his anxious cries, and we continued our perilous descent. At last, the bottom of our boat touched the dark waters below.

Seamen Humphreys and Brice, who had taken charge of our lifeboat, ordered the men to row hard and fast, away from the possible suction of the

*davit—a beam used on board ship, as a crane

sinking ship. As we inched away, I looked back at boat number thirteen descending, and a chill went up my spine. The waterline had already reached the engine room's large vent, causing the water to swirl and churn beneath the lifeboat. They were caught in a fast current that thrust them astern. The strong current created such tension on the lines that they were unable to unhook from the falls. It appeared to be impossible to pull away from the steadily sinking *Titanic*.

To make matters worse, lifeboat number fifteen was being lowered and loomed above their heads. The crew, immediately realizing the severity of the situation, shouted desperately to those above. Their cries fell on deaf ears as boat number fifteen inched closer with each passing second.

There was no time to lose. Something had to be done! Grasping his knife and leaping to the stern, a brave man took action. With the other boat just ten feet above their heads, he began to sever the thick ropes with sure, strong strokes. A seaman aboard the helpless vessel did the same at the bow. Meanwhile, the other men stood and strained with all their might, to hold the descending vessel from crushing them beneath its weight. Thankfully, and with no time to spare, they were freed of the rope, and the same current that swept them into danger, now carried them to the safety of the calm waters beyond.

Focusing back on *Titanic*, I was shocked to see that the ship had sunk halfway. Even at that point, it was hard for me to believe that the big ship was actually sinking. Most of the portholes were still lit by the electric lights, and the whole ship looked like a beacon of safety as her bright lights flickered and danced in the reflection on the water. Illuminating the vast darkness surrounding us, the Grand Lady *Titanic* sparkled as if she was naïve of her impending doom.

Calming strands of music floated down from *Titanic's* polished decks. I recognized the tune of *Nearer My God to Thee* as the band's angelic music

drifted across the still waters. It seemed that heaven was opening its doors. It was much later that I realized heaven was, indeed, opening its door that night and welcoming in all who believed in the Lord Jesus Christ.

The lights still shone brilliantly, and soft music continued to fill the night air as *Titanic's* bow sank steadily deeper into the dark waters. Then, quite unexpectedly, the stern of the great ship rose out of the water, lifting the propellers high into the air. I heard a tremendous crashing noise as if all the insides of the ship were crumbling together. The lights flickered; then went out.

For a moment, all was silent. I strained my eyes to adjust to the sudden darkness, trying my hardest to make out the form of the ship. Outlined against the starry sky, I saw the stern quickly rise until it seemed to stand on end. A horrible tearing and crashing noise shortly followed as the bow slipped beneath the waters. The stern again turned up on end. My eyes widened with amazement as I watched it bob like a cork for what seemed at least a minute or two. Then, as if the Grand Lady could hold on no longer, she plunged straight down and disappeared in the grip of the icy waters.

The seamen in our boat rowed quickly away from the place, avoiding the dangerous suction. I sat still for a long time, numb with cold and confusion, trying to understand what had just taken place. My young heart did not yet realize the gravity of it all, but I knew that it was very serious. As I peered at the dark waters where *Titanic's* lights had shone so brilliantly, all I could see was the flickering reflection of the stars.

"Are you cold, dear?" a kind-hearted woman sitting by my side asked. Until she spoke, I had hardly realized there was anyone else in the boat with me. Now I looked all about me. Auntie Jessie sat to my left and another lady to my right. But beyond that, all I could see was the outline of what looked like a huddled mass of people. I could hear some of the women crying softly.

"Dearest, are you cold?" The kind woman put a blanket around my shoulders and sweetly urged me to respond.

"Yes, ma'am. Thank you," I said with a shiver, realizing just how cold I really was.

"Is your Mama on this boat?" the lady questioned.

"No ma'am. Mother went to heaven when I was a wee baby. Father told me that she was just too sweet a lass to live on earth any longer. He said God had to bring her home with all the angels."

"Nan, darling," Auntie Jessie finally said, her voice shaking with emotion, "you must be quite weary. Why don't you just lay your head here on my lap and see if you can sleep a bit."

I started to lay down my head, but stopped when I heard a couple of seamen talking together in low voices.

"With the way this night has gone, we may bob about here for days before we are picked up—if we are picked up at all," one of them said skeptically.

"Cheer up, chap! We may yet have a chance," the older man encouraged. "In all my years at sea, I've never seen the North Atlantic as calm as this." Hearing this did not help to quiet my questioning little heart, but I obediently laid my head down on auntie's lap and closed my eyes.

Unfortunately, my heart would not rest and my mind continued to race as I recollected the events of the past hours. "What happened to all the people who were still on deck just before the lights went out?" I wondered. What if I cannot find Father's lifeboat? What if Father did not find a lifeboat at all?"

Quickly dismissing that thought, I opened my eyes and stared blankly into the night sky. All was completely dark, except for the brilliant star-strewn dome sparkling in the heavens above. I had never seen so many stars!

All at once, I remembered what Father had told me in our cabin just a few hours ago. While I gazed up at the sky Father's words whispered in my ears— almost as if he were there by my side.

"There are not only more stars than ye could ever count," Father had said, "but when you look through a telescope, there are thousands more than your natural eye can see. And yet . . . our Heavenly Father has crafted each one and knows their number."

"Whenever the cares of this world are heavy upon my heart, I often look up at the sky and remember that the God who fashioned the starry heavens is the same God who created me. There is nothing too great for Him and nothing too small. Nan, ye need not ever fear. God's Word says He has loved you with an everlasting love, and nothing can separate you from the love of Christ . . . Even in death there is victory if you have the Father's love."

Once again, a Divine peace swept over me, and closing my eyes, I thanked my Heavenly Father that He held me in the palm of His loving hand. Despite my young age, I knew Father was right, and that there was nothing that could separate me from the love of Christ—nothing!

For I am persuaded that neither death nor life,

nor angels nor principalities nor powers,

nor things present nor things to come,

nor height nor depth,

nor any other created thing,

shall be able to separate us from the love of God

which is in Christ Jesus our Lord.

Romans 8:38-39

CHAPTER SIX

A Beautiful Morning

awoke early, and, sitting up, looked all about me. The first glimmer of light began to glow on the eastern horizon. The sun rose in its quiet manner, casting its warm rays into the depths of the icy waters. Piercing through the darkness, its smiling face seemed to soften the harshness of the previous night.

I rubbed my eyes in disbelief—it seemed as if I were in a dream. All about me were ships and sailboats. Their sails looked like clouds as they floated above me. Such lovely colors, too! I had never seen sails like these—some were white, and some were soft pink and rich scarlet with hues of blue and royal purple. They even changed colors as the gentle breeze caressed their noble sails.

I became aware of a hand on my shoulder, and looking up, I remembered where I was. It was the kind lady who had given me a blanket the night before.

"Do you see all the icebergs, dear?" she asked, pointing at the great sails about me. "Are they not the most beautiful things your eyes have ever beheld?"

"Yes, ma'am," was all I could answer, as I realized that these lovely sails were actually giant icebergs!

"It is amazing that something so lovely, so incredibly beautiful, could be the cause of such a terrible disaster," she mused more to herself than to me. Her eyes drifted to the horizon where the waters and the sky blended so perfectly that it was hard to distinguish one from the other.

Fixing her eyes in the direction *Titanic* was last seen, she said, "'Tis strange that such a brief incident can alter the course of a life so drastically that it can change one's eternal perspective—even their eternal destiny."

I could not help but smile. "Eternal destiny" was a phrase that I knew quite well. If this lady had not known Christ before last night, she certainly had gained that eternal perspective of which Father so often spoke. My heart filled with joy as I thought of how happy Father would be when I told him. I still had not accepted the thought that I might never again see him on this earth.

When we made out the form of our rescue ship, *Carpathia*, all aboard the lifeboat regained hope. A burst of enthusiasm swept through our little vessel, and we all sang *Pull for Shore, Sailor*.

Father had said the night before, "It will be beautiful in the morning." And indeed it was. But the beauty I beheld was far inferior to the beauty Father saw that morning. He once said, "sudden death would be sudden glory." That morning he beheld the face of the Son of Glory and was welcomed into His eternal home.

✦ ✦ ✦ ✦ ✦ ✦ ✦ ✦ ✦ ✦ ✦ ✦ ✦

Nan paused as Gordon gently wiped away a tear that rolled down his mother's soft cheek.

"Go on, Mama dear, tell me about Grandfather's last words," Gordon tenderly urged.

"Yes, I will, darling," Nan said, smiling through her tears. "Your grandfather's last words, and the courage he displayed, have so challenged me to deepen my faith, that I now passionately long to see the salvation of others." She placed her hand on Gordon's shoulder and continued. "I can already see the godly character of my Father in you, and I would be so blessed if you grew up to be just like him. Wiping one last tear from her eye, Nan continued.

✦ ✦ ✦ ✦ ✦ ✦ ✦ ✦ ✦ ✦ ✦ ✦ ✦

It wasn't until years later that I came across accounts of *Titanic's* sinking, written by survivors who mentioned Father. To my delight, some people even sought out our family, just to tell us how much Father had blessed their lives. As the stories trickled in, I was eventually able to put all the pieces together and understand what my father experienced right before he met His Savior face-to-face.

After Father and I said good-bye, he helped as many women and children as possible to board the lifeboats, until the last vessel safely reached the waters below. Then, Father approached a crewman without a life-vest and insisted upon giving him his own.

"I'm not going down, sir—I'm going up!" Father said with peaceful assurance. Then he made his way to the band and requested that they play *Nearer My God to Thee*. As the band began to play the sweet strands of music, Father knelt down in the midst of some men who had gathered and began to pray. With his arms lifted toward the heavens and his upturned face full of Christ's presence, he thanked God that he would soon see Him face-to-face and asked for mercy for the souls of those around him.

Before *Titanic* sank two and a half miles to the ocean floor, Father jumped off the ship and was trying his hardest to swim, despite the freezing waters. A man clinging to driftwood floated past him. Though the driftwood could have saved his life, Father thought only of the other man's eternal salvation.

"Man, are ye saved?" Father called into the darkness.

"No, I am not," came the desperate reply.

"Believe on the Lord Jesus Christ, and thou shalt be saved!" Father's voice trailed off, as a current drifted them apart. The man, clinging to the driftwood, recognized Father as the preacher who had witnessed to him on the second-class deck just hours before the ship had struck the iceberg. He was amazed that out of over two thousand passengers, he should meet up with the preacher again. He was still more amazed when, minutes later, Father swam by a second time.

"Are ye saved?" he cried out again.

Still the young man answered, "I cannot honestly say that I am."

"Believe on the Lord Jesus Christ, and thou shalt be saved."

✦ ✦ ✦ ✦ ✦ ✦ ✦ ✦ ✦ ✦ ✦ ✦ ✦

Nan looked lovingly into her young son's eyes. "Those were the last words Father ever spoke. The young man was later rescued by the *Carpathia* and lived to tell the story. He stood in a church meeting in New York two weeks later and declared that he was John Harper's last convert. Though Father was reported lost when *Titanic's* passengers were listed, his soul was saved, and he has left us a lasting legacy that will never die.

Conclusion

Over fifteen hundred people perished that night beneath the chilling waters of the North Atlantic. Like John Harper, many men died as heroes, giving their lives for the women and children aboard the ship.

John Jacob Astor, one of the wealthiest men in the world, willingly gave up his seat in the lifeboat for a third-class washerwoman. To encourage those who were about to face their Maker, band leader, Wallace Hartley, played Christian hymns until the water covered his knees. More than sixty cabin boys and stewards chose to step back and allow women and children to leave *Titanic* in the safety of the lifeboats—all sixty perished that night.

There were also many noble women who showed courage and strength in the face of death. Ida Strauss remained with her husband, Isidor, to the end. She was heard to say "We have been . . . together for many years. Where you go, I go."

First-class passenger, Edith Evans, insisted on giving up her spot on the lifeboat to a third-class mother with young children.

The Scottish Countess of Rothes was saved, and without her courageous actions, lifeboat number eight may not have made it to the *Carpathia*. In the absence of enough seamen aboard the lifeboat, the gracious countess was asked to man the tiller, and she rowed all night without complaint.

All of these men and women will be remembered for their sacrifice and bravery displayed during the disaster. They are an ever-present reminder that "greater love hath no man than this, that a man lay down his life for his friends."

Nan never forgot the sinking of *Titanic*, nor the legacy of faith that her father had left behind. She safely returned to Scotland with her Auntie Jessie. Upon graduation from high school, Nan attended Bible college in England and followed her father's example as she devoted herself to full-time ministry in the inner cities of England. Nan and her husband, Reverend Philip Roy Pont, committed their lives to serving the Lord and raising their children for God's glory.

Call upon Me in the day of trouble;

I will deliver you, and you shall glorify Me.

Psalm 50:15

Author's Notes

Nan and her aunt, Jessie Leitch, were among the few who were saved. More than half of *Titanic's* passengers died that night. Many lifeboats were not filled to their capacity, and amazingly enough, some were too afraid to board them. They did not want to leave the "safety" of the giant ship and trust in the frail little boats, which looked so small compared to the enormous, "unsinkable" *Titanic*.

This is so often the case in our own lives. We would much rather find security in what our mind thinks is "safe." As Nan and her father, John Harper, knew, it is not until we leap into the "lifeboat of faith" in the Lord

Jesus Christ that we will be saved. Taking a leap of faith is not always the easiest when you have been sailing on the "ship of deception." When your journey has been filled with the lavish comforts of a self-centered mindset and the allure of worldly pursuits, it is hard to leave the "gold" of intellectual pride. But as *Titanic* survivors soon discovered, boarding a modest vessel was the only thing that would save their lives. The "lifeboat of faith" in God will include, at times, rough waters and personal sacrifice, but when your journey of faith reaches its final destination, eternal peace and joy await you.

When the lifeboats reached the *Carpathia*, some passengers were too cold to climb up the ladders, but they were not abandoned. The captain of the ship let down some net harnesses and lifted them to safety. It is the same with our lives on a daily basis aboard the vessel of faith. Our Heavenly Father is always there to lift us up in His arms of grace. All we need to do is look up with eyes of faith, remembering that nothing can separate us from the love of Christ.